ETIENNE DELESSERT

ASHES ASHES

STEWART, TABORI & CHANG

FOR IMMEDIATE RELEASE
September 1990

CONTACT: Claudia Guerra
(212) 941-2988

ASHES, ASHES

WRITTEN AND ILLUSTRATED BY
ETIENNE DELESSERT

Etienne Delessert's latest journey into the world of creativity — **ASHES, ASHES** published by Stewart, Tabori & Chang, $14.95 August — is a fantastic passage to the realm of the imagination and ultimately, self-discovery.

The cadence and content of Delessert's free verse is mirrored in the imagery and composition of his 25 full-color illustrations. Warm shadows and subtle lines, familiar territory and fantastic turns, invite the reader to join in the exploration of a surreal new world.

At the urging of three strangers, an adventurous youth embarks on a pilgrimage for truth and purity. Shedding his identity, he is transformed into an imaginary animal-like being with long furry ears and a pointed nose, *"a yaketifish or a bully bear,"* a whimsical creature that is sure to delight childrens' fancies.

Dissatisfied with his ugly and uninspired surroundings, he leaves *"this world with holes in the sky, with mountains of rusted waste and green raindrops,"* for a land where egg-shaped rocks are soft and cold streams can be burning.

On his journey he finds other youths like him. Together they build a community and rely on nature to fill their needs.

Industriously, they cultivate the land with turkey feathers, gather bouquets, and build a dam. Then the days grow dark and long from a fog which settles over the stilled water and the youth realizes he must return to the world he left behind in order to continue his search.

A delightful, many-layered celebration of the imagination, **ASHES, ASHES** is sure to become a classic journey tale.

ETIENNE DELESSERT was born in 1941 near Lausanne in Switzerland and today lives in Connecticut. Delessert is a painter and author of more than forty children's books. His work has twice been awarded the prestigious Graphics Prize at the Bologna Children's Book Fair.

ASHES, ASHES
25 full-color illustrations
32 pages, 8 1/2 x 11"
Cloth, jacketed; $14.95 (U.S.) $18.95 (Canada)
ISBN: 1-55670-137-3
Publication Date: August 1990

FOR FURTHER INFORMATION, CONTACT: Claudia Guerra or Alexander Smithline, Publicity Department, Stewart, Tabori & Chang, 575 Broadway, New York, NY 10012, (212) 941-2988.

For Adrien

Copyright ©1990 Etienne Delessert
Designed by Rita Marshall

Published in 1990 by
Stewart, Tabori & Chang, Inc.
740 Broadway, New York, New York 10003

Library of Congress Cataloging-in-Publication Data

Delessert, Etienne.
   Ashes, ashes / Etienne Delessert.
      p.   cm.
Summary: A youngster's search for purity and truth
leads him to sharing a communal life with new
friends and then back again to the real world.
   ISBN 1-55670-137-3
   I. Title.   89-28586
PZ7.D3832As   1990   CIP
(Fic) – dc20   AC

Distributed in the U.S. by Workman Publishing,
708 Broadway, New York, New York 10003

Distributed in Canada by Canadian Manda Group,
P.O. Box 920 Station U, Toronto, Ontario M8Z 5P9

Distributed in all other territories by
Little, Brown and Company, International Division,
34 Beacon Street, Boston, Massachusetts 02108

Printed in Japan   10 9 8 7 6 5 4 3 2 1

ASHES ASHES

by Etienne Delessert

Stewart, Tabori & Chang
New York

*A*s I came across the lake
– for I was over there –
a thin lady waited for me
with dried flowers.

We walked through town,
met a sad old friend.
"Not much to say," he mumbled.
"It's dark at high noon.
Anyway, I have to go.

"Do you hear the horn?
Do you hear the song?"
"Yes," I said.
"Yes," she said.
And I headed home alone
holding my violin tight.

Three men stood on the front porch,
their faces very pale.
They swayed in their long black coats,
and they hummed:
"Do you hear the horn?
Do you hear the song?
Long, long was our journey.
Wind and rain caked the dust on our shoes.
Long, long is the journey.
We will not rest before our coats turn white,
the color of ashes in an old cold fire.

"Long, long furry ears
and pointed nose,
you'll be a yaketifish
or a bullybear,
until you find the truth."

The air had the bitter taste of iron.
I wasn't afraid.
Maybe I had known for years
this would happen.
"Shed your skin," said the song,
"change your name, wash your face away.
Leave this world with holes in the sky,
with mountains of rusted waste
and green raindrops.
Fly, fly away
from whirling tornadoes,
from cracked and opened earth."

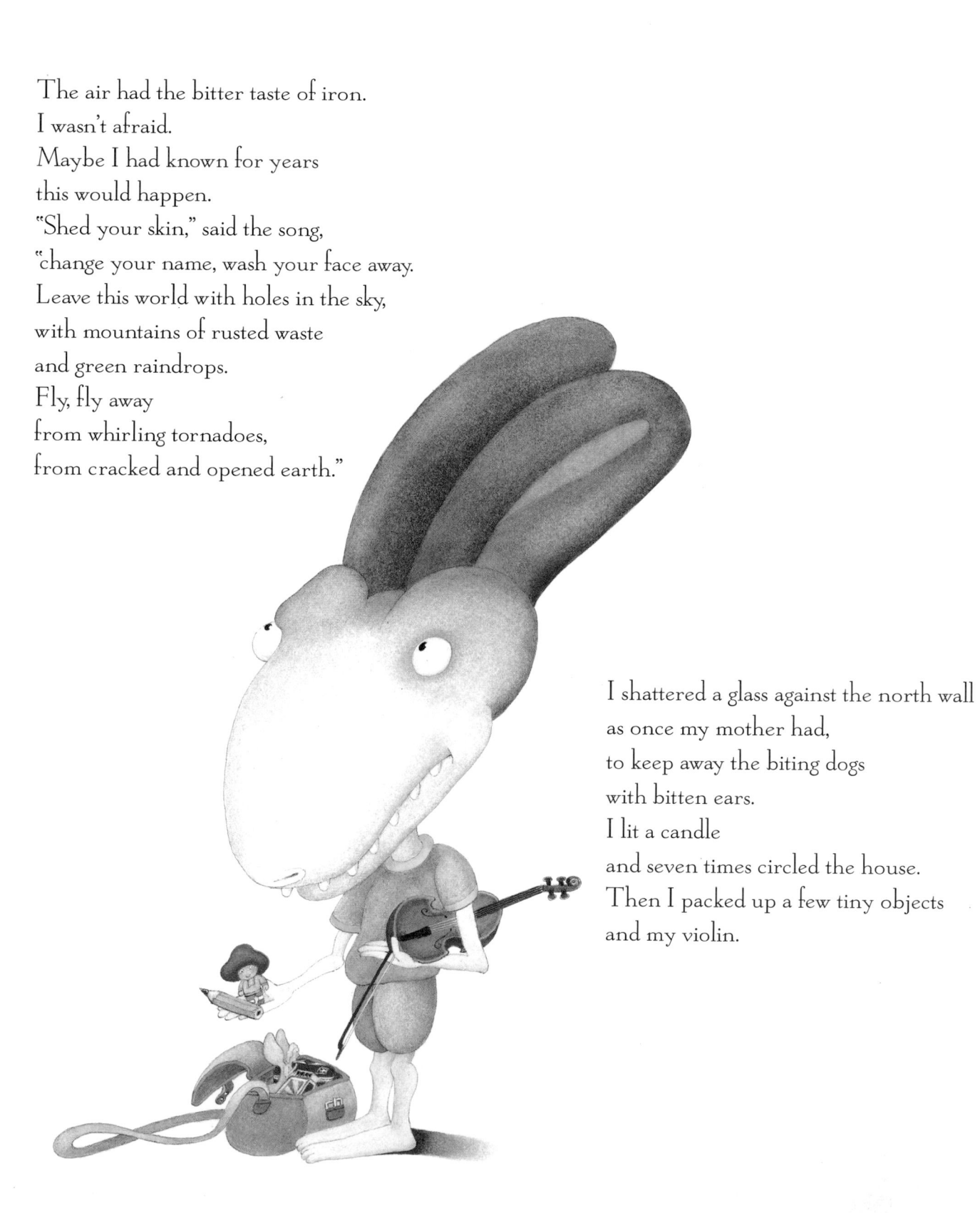

I shattered a glass against the north wall
as once my mother had,
to keep away the biting dogs
with bitten ears.
I lit a candle
and seven times circled the house.
Then I packed up a few tiny objects
and my violin.

Wrapped in seven clouds
of soft, powdery silver
I headed over hills and across muddy rivers
to the land where I could be alone,
and plow the fields,
pick wrinkled apples,
wash in fresh spring water.
There even the dust would taste sweet,
like white flour on warm oatmeal bread.

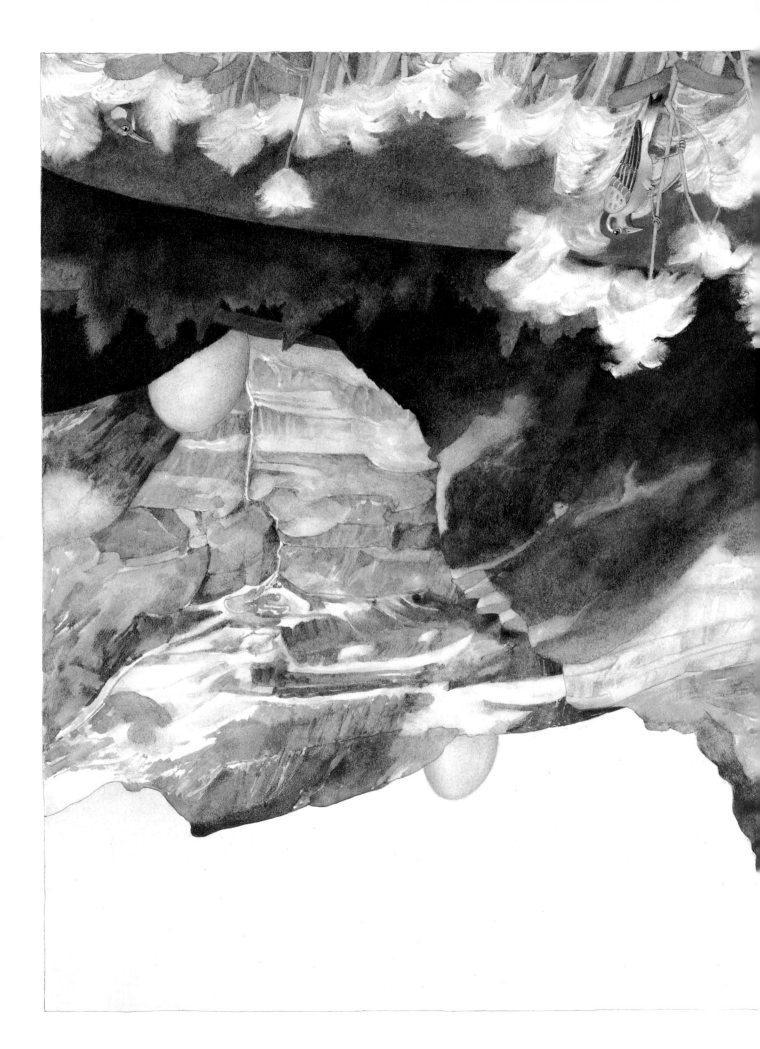

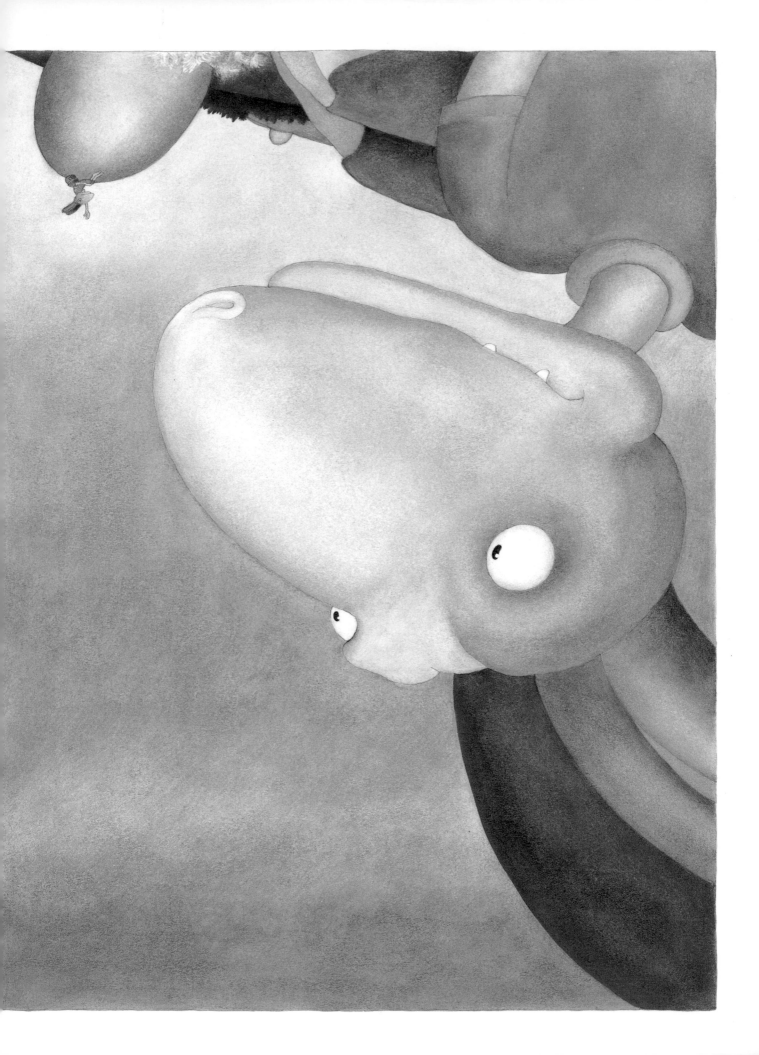

I landed on a soft, round rock.
But I wasn't alone.
"What's your name?" he called.
I didn't know,
I didn't answer.

We slid down the polished slopes
and sat together by a pond.
I told him about the three pale men
and he nodded as I dusted silver
from his shoulder.
I showed him my violin and my picture;
he took a red button and tiny mirror
from his pocket.

Then we skimmed pebbles
and ate wild strawberries.
He asked me to play a tune
about the yellowing sky,
the long shadows,
how we shed our skins,
changed our faces,
washed our names away.

We were tired
so we found a place
in one of the round rocks.
We made a nest of grass and cottonweed
and peonies.
We watched the clouds erase the moon.

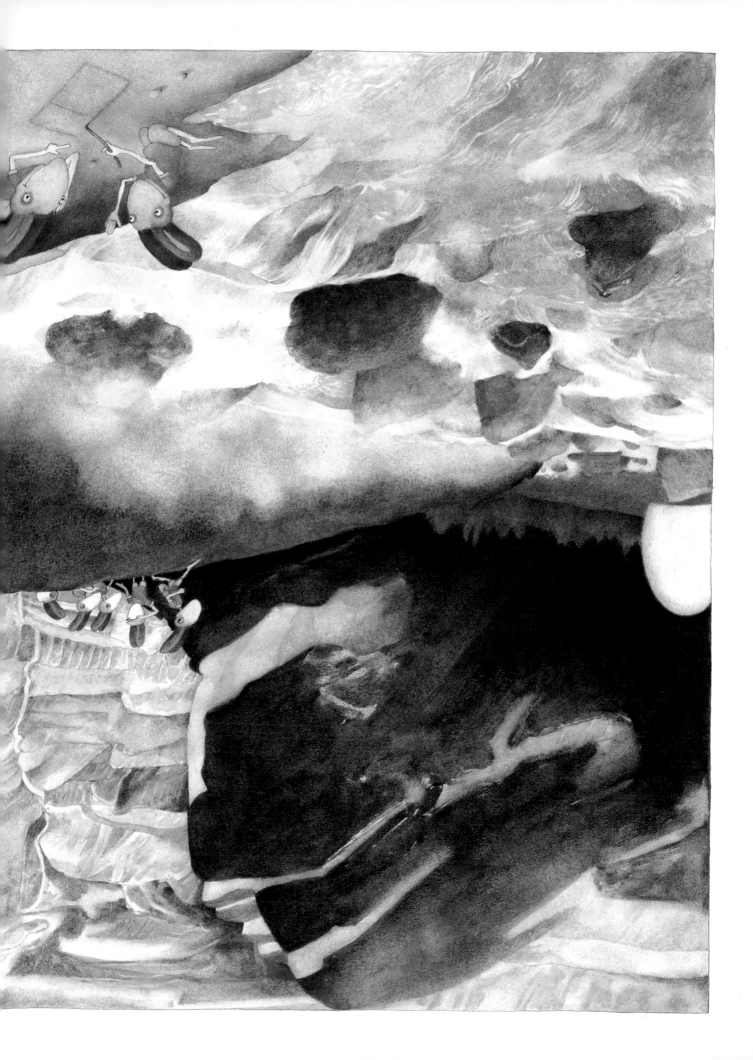

Awakened by the sun
we splashed in a burning cold stream.
There was a trout hiding under a stone,
and a salamander.
I found some cookies in my bag.
I smiled at my new friend.

We decided to build a house
and drew plans in wet sand:
one room for me,
one room for him,
and a room for us to play.

Since we were busy
we didn't hear them coming.
Five of them
– seven of us –
all with a silver shine on our clothes.

They offered us some soft, sweet nuts,
and we made plans for five more rooms.
Then, high on a cliff, away from the wind,
we found a place for the house.

We chased wild turkeys
and ate blackberries.
I built a cage to keep our fire alive,
and we grilled fish on a thin, flat stone.
As the sun set behind the hill
I played my violin for my new friends.
We curled up in the cottonweed,
deep in the round rock.

In two weeks the house was finished.
We made every shape simple
and glued the joints with honey.
Each in his own room, we spent our first day
alone
quietly thanking the three pale men
who told us of the journey
and brought us together as friends.

Later we met in the playroom
to dance and shake and twirl and jump,
giggling round and round the room,
faster and up in the air.

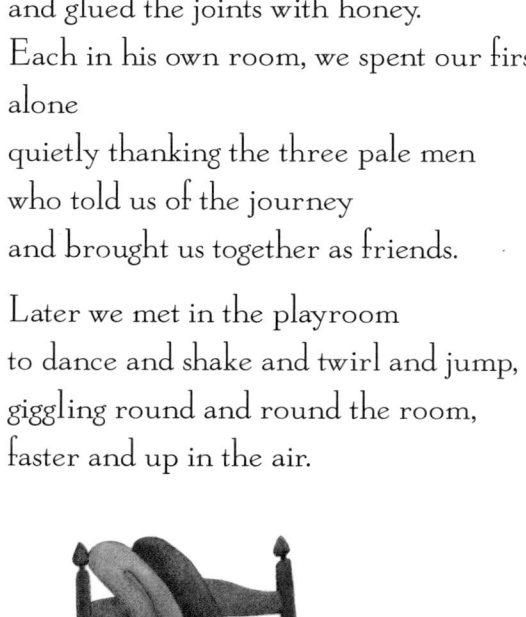

We spun outside and lay down
dizzy in the moonshine,
listening to the cicadas creaking in the trees.

One day we found a patch
where the dirt was dark and moist.
We remembered the color of wheat
and opened
a field of parallel furrows.
Small birds followed us in the haze,
picking bugs and squiggly worms.
We planted hundreds of tiny turkey feathers
and sprinkled them with a pinch
of our precious silver powder.

Every morning,
every evening,
a slice of fish,
a sliver of turkey,
some berries and cherries.
For green
we chewed mint and sage.
For red,
rosebuds and nasturtiums.
For blue,
we watched the edges of the sky.

We built a dam,
rolled heavy rocks,
pushed mud and clay,
carried fallen trees
so wild things would grow in the deep water.
As the tall birch trees slowly disappeared
in the rising lake,
ducks settled in the high branches.
We felt gray and damp in the morning fog.
I didn't play my violin.

Every day we gathered bouquets,
every day collected shiny black marbles,
every day carved whistles for the birds
and sat in silence by the lake
looking at ripples that came and went
on the dull water.
We skimmed pebbles
again
and watched them sink.
We dressed in costume
but it wasn't much fun.
No longer were the mornings
crisp and clear.
A dense fog always covered the lake,
melting the trees and rocks in the valley.
The days were so long.

I heard the horn calling me again
one day before the sun rose.
I took my violin
and left the house
where my friends were still asleep.
I followed the music
in the thick, damp air.
Feeling very small, but daring too,
I climbed between the rocks
on the slippery grass.

The horn was distant, soft and deep.
My violin sounded pure and sweet
as I played my own song:
"Goodbye to the valley,
goodbye lake and pale roses,
goodbye crops of wilted feathers
and bird whistles.
Goodbye my friends
with your long funny ears."

They were my friends.
But they were strangers, too.
I enjoyed being together.
I had wanted to be alone.
But the three men never reappeared.
I would have shared the fish with them.
We could have chased turkeys.
I had saved my last cookie for them.

I had invented a new song.
But the words no longer rhymed.
And the silver dust was gone.

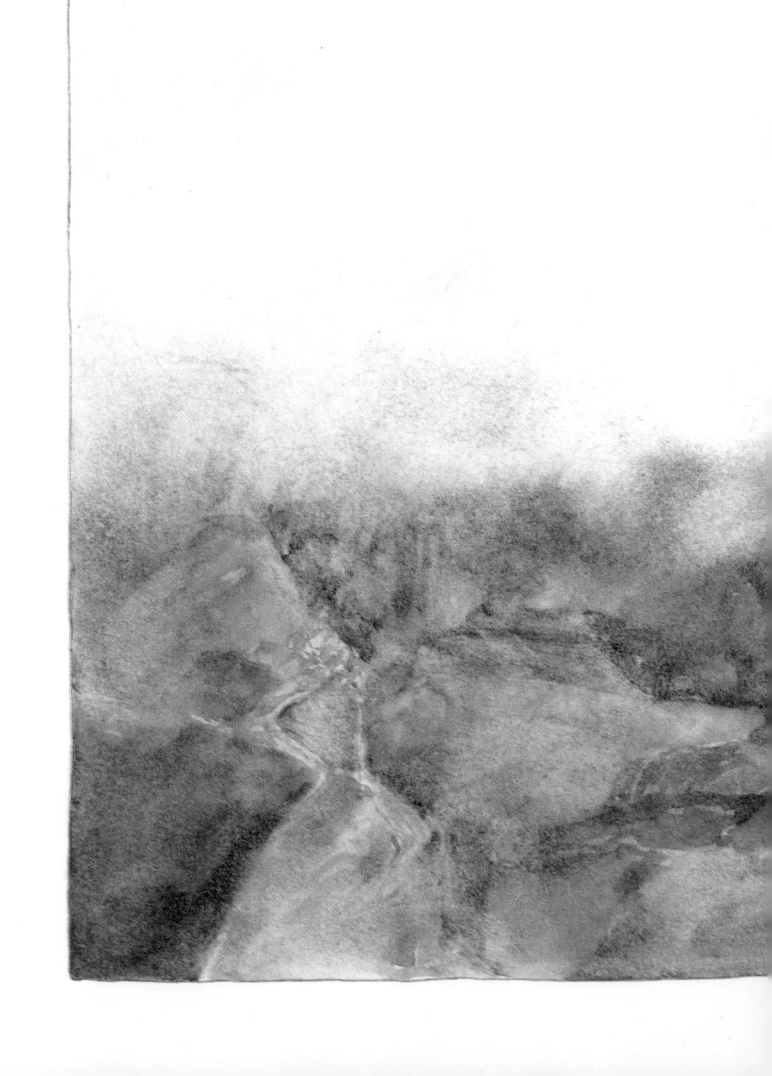

I reached the first patches of snow
and could barely hear the horn anymore.
So I played my own song
loud.
The fog parted in front of me.

And I came across the lake
where a thin lady waited for me
with dried flowers and a soft smile.

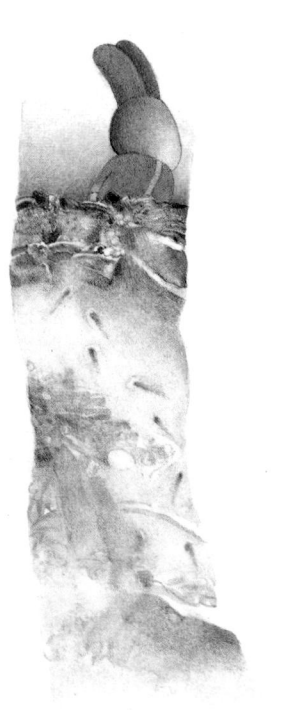